The Body in the Bookstore

A Very Merry Murder Mystery, Volume 3

Rachel Beattie

Published by Rachel Beattie, 2024.

This is a work of fiction. Similarities to real people, places, or events are entirely coincidental.

THE BODY IN THE BOOKSTORE

First edition. July 12, 2024.

Copyright © 2024 Rachel Beattie.

ISBN: 979-8224232048

Written by Rachel Beattie.

Chapter One

"What a beautiful little coffee shop!"

As soon as I hear Cassandra Clinton's voice, time stands still. Don't get me wrong, Aunt Cassie and I talk to each other a lot. We message back and forth at least a few times a week and now that she's discovered voice-memos I regularly get a detailed verbal run-down of her latest opinion of whatever reality show we're both invested in or an in-depth description of her current neighbor-intrigue. But it's not often we actually get a chance to be together in person, so when the door to the Jitterbug Junction swings open and she steps inside it's like a breath of fresh air.

"Meredith! Come give me a hug!"

I obediently run around the front of the counter and am gathered up in a floral embrace from one of my favorite people in the entire world.

"What are you doing here?" I ask when she finally lets me go. "I thought your train wasn't getting in until later. I was going to close up early and come pick you up."

"I know, I know." She nods her head, making her bobbed grey hair bounce. "But I was ready to come and there didn't see any point in killing time alone in Patterson when I could spend it with you! And I didn't need collecting. Do you think I'm incapable of finding my way here from the train station?"

"Where's your luggage?" I frown at her and that's when she laughs and admits the truth.

"Oh, very well! I persuaded a very nice man called Edward to drive me up here. He's waiting outside and said if I could get your keys we'll take my bags straight to your house!"

"Cassie!" I burst out of the door and see a very old car spitting fumes while its engine idles noisily.

"You must be the niece!" A man who is somehow even older than his car leans out of the driver's side window and salutes me. "Pleasure to meet you!"

"And you are?"

"Eddie." He grins toothily at me and I glance over my shoulder at my aunt, who's beaming at her new would-be conquest.

"Come on, let's get your bags out here. I have my car so we can leave them in the trunk and then take them home later."

"You sure?" Eddie asks, his smile fading. "S'really no trouble..."

"I'm sure." I move around to the back of the car and with a sigh Eddie pops the trunk, revealing a bright pink suitcase and a matching floral day bag that I would have picked out as belonging to my aunt anywhere. I slide the bag over my shoulder and lift out the suitcase before carefully closing the trunk and wincing as it crunches shut. "Thank you so much."

Eddie is evidently angling for something more than a dismissal from my Aunt Cassie, and her eyes sparkle merrily at me before she turns and blows him a kiss goodbye.

"Be seein' you..." He eases the car back onto the street and slowly disappears in a coughing, spluttering cloud of exhaust fumes.

"What?" Aunt Cassie shrugs her shoulders as if this was the most normal thing in the world. Which it probably is, in her world. "You think you're the only girl who can find a cute guy around here?"

"Cute?" I splutter and Cassie laughs, taking the handle of her suitcase from my hand and dragging it behind her. We reach my car and I pop the trunk, clearing as much space as I can for her belongings, and wince at the amount of trash I've been carrying around.

"What I want to know is when I can expect to meet *your* new man."

I carefully wedge her luggage inside and gingerly close the trunk over it, letting out a sigh of relief as I hear the lock catch. I'm grateful to not be looking at her right then because I can feel my cheeks heat at the mention of my *new man*. It's early days, but my relationship with Silver Brook's most eligible vet is going pretty well. So well, I'm almost sorry he isn't going to be here to meet my aunt while she's in town. Then I recall how much of a challenge she can be when she wants to and I think he's got the better end of the deal.

"He's away at a conference this week," I say, apologetically. "Exotic animals."

"What, there aren't enough of those here in Silver Brook?" Cassie spots a vaguely familiar figure loping down the street towards us and her voice drops, along with all the brightness in her eyes. "Such as..."

"Morning, Merry!"

Ugh. My ex-husband Neil and I have gotten pretty good at tolerating each other lately, but that doesn't mean I enjoy it when our paths cross. I fold my arms and watch as the recognition dawns on his face, wiping away his jaunty smile. He glances across the street and I see him wish he hadn't walked this way but it's too late now and it would be rude not to at least acknowledge someone he knows. Or *knew*.

"Cassie! Wh-what are you doing here?"

"Visiting my niece." Cassie slides an arm around my waist and draws herself up to her full height next to me. "What are you doing here?"

"I live here." Neil glances at me as if for assistance. "And I...I was just going to grab a coffee." His cheeks flush guiltily and I take pity on him.

"Fine, come on in. I'm certainly not going to say no to good business."

I hear Cassie mutter something else as we head back towards the Jitterbug but I decide to leave Neil to fend that one off by himself. Even though we are more-or-less amicable these days I don't see why he shouldn't have to suffer a little now and then.

"Hasn't Merry done a marvelous job with this place?" Cassie asks, throwing her arms wide as if to encompass the whole of the Jitterbug Junction, the most popular cafe in all of Silver Brook. "It's charming!"

"That's thanks to Maggie," I say, thinking of the friend who built this business up from nothing. She got an offer of a job elsewhere and offered it to me and honestly, I couldn't be happier with my new life. A new boyfriend (even if he is out of town this week) a new job, and now my favorite aunt is in town for a visit. Later today we'll get to go to a book launch for the latest novel penned by one of our shared favorite crime writers, Aloysius Hunt.

"Don't sell yourself short, Merry," Neil says, with a wary look in Cassie's direction. "You've made this place your own." He nods to the vases of flowers on every table and smiles. "You always did like daisies."

"You'll want a latte?" I ask, abruptly making my way to the coffee machine. Just because Neil and I can tolerate each other doesn't mean I want to stand around and reminisce with him. Especially not when I can feel my aunt's eyes fixed on me, watching every micro-reaction as if hunting for clues. *That's probably exactly what she is doing*, I think, as I bustle about getting Neil's coffee ready. *When I told her about the book launch she joked that it was about time she was here to try her hand at solving a murder instead of leaving me to have all the fun.* I shudder, thinking that *fun* was the very last adjective I'd apply to my experiences recently in Silver Brook.

"So, are you excited about the book launch?"

I jump, sloshing hot milk over the edge of the cup, and turn to glare at Neil, who's extricated himself from Cassie's inquisition and come to make conversation with me instead, assuming I'll be a bit easier to get along with. I take a moment to wipe my hands before turning towards him and bite back the urge to scowl. Some time ago I decided not to let bitterness and resentment towards my ex-husband eat me up inside, but sometimes it's harder to remember that than others. Especially when he's leaning across the counter with that particular grin of his.

"He's one of your favorites, isn't he? The mystery writer?"

I nod, surprised and a little touched that he remembers this. I pass him his latte and allow him to pay for it. Letting go of resentment is one thing, but only real friends get freebies.

"Peter's asked me to cater." I wince. "My first proper catering job since taking over this place. I mean, it's only cupcakes, but..."

"Hey, good for you!" Neil's smile is genuine this time, and I carefully return it as he makes his way towards the door. "And I hope you enjoy your visit, Cassie!"

My aunt waves at him imperiously but her gaze is fixed on me and it's absolutely no surprise when she comes tottering up to the counter to quiz me.

"What did he want?"

"Coffee." I wipe down the counter and reach for my phone, surprised I haven't been more inundated with customers yet. We're in a lull, but even so it's suspiciously quiet for a regular Silver Brook morning. I'm just beginning to fret when the door swings open and Peter Stalker marches in, his features scrunched with stress and anxiety.

"Meredith! Where are those cupcakes you promised me? I thought you were going to deliver them to me on time!"

"I was," I protest. "I am! But you didn't want them arriving too early." I repeat his words back to him. "You didn't want them sitting around cluttering up the place before Mr Hunt arrived. You said two o'clock." I angle my phone towards him so he can see the time. "It's not even eleven yet."

"Did I?" Peter runs an absent-minded hand through his thinning grey hair. "Yes, yes. Well. As long as you haven't forgotten."

"I haven't." I smile tightly. It seems like I inherited Peter Stalker's long-standing grudge against Maggie when I took on her business, and I'm fairly sure if he could have found anyone else to cater for today's book launch he'd have done so. *But this is my first gig*, I remind myself. *It has to go well.* I swallow, trying to fit my voice with a brightness I don't naturally feel. "Would you like to take them with you now?"

Peter frowns, then nods.

"Yes, I'd better. Then there's no chance of them being forgotten." He looks at me expectantly and I hurry around to the kitchen, piling several boxes on top of one another and gingerly bringing them back through to him. He looks a little shocked that there are so many but I forestall his criticism.

"This is exactly what you ordered. Can you manage?"

"Erm...yes. Yes, thank you." He holds his arms out and I ease the boxes into them, making it almost impossible for him to see over the top.

"Here, let me get the door for you," I say, in an abundance of sweetness as I help him out of the shop. "And I'll see you in a few hours. My aunt has come to town especially for your event, and we're very excited to meet Mr Hunt!"

"Oh! Well...excellent. Yes." Peter turns, trying and failing to make out Aunt Cassie and in the end he abandons the attempt, focusing his attention instead on making it safely back to his bookshop with the leaning tower of cupcake trays safely in one piece. The door swings closed behind him and I let out a breath.

"I'd give odds on those cupcakes surviving the journey," Cassie remarks, fighting a smile. "I hope he already paid you for them."

I open my mouth but before I can even begin to reply a bloodcurdling shriek pierces the quiet morning.

Chapter Two

I bolt out into the street and can feel Aunt Cassie hot on my heels, but we don't make it more than a few steps before we see the source of the commotion. A young man is struggling to stand upright, weighted down on all sides with bags and clutching a box so tall he can scarcely see over it. Peter Stalker had the same problem, and they both narrowly avoided a collision, but it's not Peter doing the yelling, as I first thought. Another man is standing a few feet away, one hand clutched at his chest as if he, and not his young friend, narrowly avoided disaster.

"Is that...?"

I nod, recognizing the older man at the same time as my aunt does. Aloysius Hunt looks different in the flesh than in his author pictures, but there's no mistaking that superior brow - even though it's currently wrinkled in a fierce frown as he berates his young companion for not watching where he was going.

"You need to take care of other people's belongings, Patrick! And my books! What kind of a launch event would it be if the books are ruined?"

"Let me carry them."

A young woman comes to join them and eases the box out of her friend's hands. They exchange a look of relief and the young man squares his shoulders, shuffling multiple bag straps into a more comfortable position.

"Thank you, Phoebe." Hunt offers her an obsequious smile before scowling at the young man. "I'm glad one of you is taking this seriously. Come on, let's keep moving. I want time to set up and acquaint myself with the space before it gets crowded with people."

The three bustle on towards the bookshop following the route Peter Stalker took with his cupcakes and I glance at Cassie, surprised to see her usually open, cheerful face puckered in distaste.

"I'm sure he's just anxious about the book launch," I say, steering her back into the cafe. I know my aunt, and she's a stickler for politeness. The last thing I want is for her opinion of Aloysius Hunt to plummet right before we go and see him speak.

"That's no excuse not to be kind," she says, with a sniff.

"You're right." I smile and feel a little convicted that I haven't actually made her anything to eat or drink yet. "You must be hungry after traveling. What can I get you?"

Cassie takes my arm and strolls with me up to the counter where she beams at the glass cabinet stuffed to the brim with pastries, cookies, and freshly baked muffins.

"One of those!" She raps an elegant French-manicured nail against the glass. "And an English Breakfast tea, please, dear."

I hastily throw together her order, thinking that something sweet will certainly soften my aunt's temper and reminding myself that she's still recovering from her long journey here. I'm tempted to join her but before I can brew a drink for myself the door swings open and a crowd of excited middle-aged ladies bustles into the cafe.

"What an adorable little coffee shop!" One coos.

"So cute! These flowers!"

"And smell that!" Another takes a noisy inhalation. "Coffee and vanilla. The perfect combination."

They're all chattering at once as they make their way towards the counter and I exchange a glance with my aunt, who is watching the new arrivals with interest.

"Good morning!" I call, taking my position by the cash register. "How can I help you today?"

"Oh, we're just admiring your lovely little cafe!" The first one beams at me. "The Jitterbug Junction! Such a cute name!" She performs an elegant little shuffle that I presume is a jitterbug dance step and her friends clap admiringly. "Well, girls. Eleanor, shall we risk cake?"

"Risk?" One of the group, a stout lady with salt-and-pepper curls tuts. "There's no risk about it, June. Look at these treats! It would be criminal to pass them by without sampling...is that raspberry roulade?"

"It is." I pick up a pair of tongs, ready to start plating up their choices, and soon everybody is bickering over their decision. In the end, everyone chooses something different, with noisy plans to share them all, and I'm handing over cakes and coffees almost faster than I can make them.

The crowd of visitors attracts a crowd of regulars, and soon the Jitterbug Junction is hopping with late-morning trade. I'm rushed off my feet and it's not until my Aunt Cassie appears next to me that I even remember she's there.

"Let me help you out, dear," she said, sliding her glasses onto her nose and peering at the cash register. "You can't do this all by yourself. Don't you have any other staff?"

"Not at the moment," I mutter, holding my breath while I pour milk foam into a perfect spiral. "I'm waiting to find the right person."

"Well, if this carries on, you might just have to take the next person who comes along." She pats me warmly on the cheek and takes the cappuccino I've perfected out of my hands, dumping a heavy measure of cocoa powder on top and thrusting it towards a customer. "Fortunately, I'm here to help for now."

"Thank you, Auntie," I say, winking at the bemused customer, who exchanges the cappuccino he didn't order with his neighbor's chamomile tea, and they both go away cheerful.

We figure out a sort-of routine where I relegate Cassie to the cash register and taking the orders that I make up and together manage to only mess up about every third one. She's not wrong that I could do with some help but I'm not convinced my chatty, enthusiastic aunt is the right person for the job.

"Hello, there!"

The most enthusiastic of the cake-eating visitors approaches me, beaming from behind her round glasses. She gives me a little wave.

"Can I get you something else?" I ask with a smile. "More roulade?"

"Don't tempt me!" She chuckles and passes me an empty coffee cup. "I'll just take another vanilla latte if you don't mind." She carefully rearranges an armful of intricately beaded bracelets and hops from one foot to another while I fix her drink.

"Are you new to Silver Brook?" I ask, trying to place her and her friends in my knowledge of my hometown. I think I would have remembered if I'd seen them before, and there aren't many people who live here who don't already know the Jitterbug Junction well.

"Just visiting." She beams at me. "We're going to see Aloysius Hunt launch his new book this afternoon at that adorable little book shop down the street." She leans in, as if confiding a secret. "I've heard it's going to be his best one yet."

"Really?" I glance at Cassie, who is deeply involved in a discussion with another customer and is oblivious to our conversation. I try to lean past her to reach the cash register but she's blocking me, and in the end I hand over the latte to my new friend without ringing it up. "I'm glad to hear that! My aunt and I are long-time fans of his."

"Oh, so are we!" The older woman points to her table of friends. "We travel all around America going to see him when he does events like this." She sighs. "Not that there's been many of those lately. Not since..."

"Not since what, dear?" Cassie's not as oblivious as I thought, and she turns abruptly to join us at the merest hint of gossip. "Just a latte, was it?" She hits a few keys on the cash register and takes payment for the drink. "Here you go." She hands the woman her change. "What were you saying about Mr Hunt? He hasn't been doing as many events lately?"

"No." The woman shakes her head and then takes a sip of her drink. "Well, you see, he's been getting all these death threats..."

"Death threats?" I roll my eyes. "That's a little bit on-brand for a crime writer, isn't it?"

My new friend doesn't laugh and I realise that there's more to this story than a bit of PR spin.

"I suppose when you're as successful as Mr Hunt is you attract all kinds of followers." Cassie shoots me a knowing look. "And not necessarily all good ones. Didn't one of his books feature a poison pen letter writer?"

"An Ink-lination to Murder."

Another of the Superfans - as I'm going to start referring to them in my head - comes to join us and I make up another latte for her while she and Cassie reminisce over Aloysius Hunt's exhaustive backlist.

"They do say art imitates life," I say, trying to break up an argument rapidly heating up between them about whether or not the poison pen letter writer in question was a red herring or a foiled murderer. "Here you are! And I don't think I've read that one."

"Oh! Well, then you certainly won't want any spoilers." The woman gives me a comical wink, takes her latte and her friend, and scoots back towards their table, leaving me and Cassie to exchange a weary smile.

"And I thought we were obsessed," I say under my breath.

"I guess there's fans and then there's *fans*," Cassie agrees, helping herself to a solitary pastry as she bustles about restoring order to the counter area. "Not that either of us should complain. They've just about cleared you out of cupcakes and cookies." She pats the cash register affectionately. "Swelled the coffers nicely."

"Still, I'm glad they're only going to be in town for today," I remark, as several voices raise in pitch and volume and another argument breaks out about Aloysius Hunt's complex characterization and difficult-to-untangle plots. "And I hope they saved some space for the cupcakes I baked for Peter Stalker." I bite my lip, wondering if he'll try to get a refund if the assembled crowd doesn't make a dent in the baked goods he purchased from me for the day. "He can be a bit funny at times."

"Funny?" Cassie looks at me with a frown and I can see her deciding whether she needs to add Peter Stalker to the list Neil's on and switch to actively disliking him on my account. I force myself to smile.

"He cares a lot about his bookstore." I gesture around us. "Like I do about this place. There's nothing he wouldn't do to make his store a success. I don't even know how he persuaded Aloysius Hunt to come to town. Silver Brook isn't exactly the bustling big city." My smile falters. I've seen first-hand how little trade Peter's bookstore does on a daily basis. How *did* he persuade a popular author like Hunt to choose that as his launch location?

Chapter Three

B y the time Cassie and I close up the cafe and hurry down
the street to the book shop, there's a crowd already forming
outside the door.

"Hurry up, Merry!" Cassie slides her arm through mine and
pulls me along beside her until I'm practically jogging to keep up.
"We need to check on those cupcakes of yours!" She shoots an
apologetic smile at the queue of guests we neatly side-step and
forces me through the door ahead of her. "The Jitterbug Junction
is exclusively catering for this event, after all!"

"Cassie!" I laugh, as we break through the crush of people
and into the relative peace of Peter Stalker's book shop. "He
already took the cupcakes. My work here is done."

"You know that," my aunt says, with a wink. "And I know
that, but why not use a little artistic license as an excuse to get
in here early? Besides, there are a lot of visitors to town. This
bookstore isn't the only small business that could do with a boost
in trade. And now we're here ahead of the crowd, we can get a
good seat!" She points to the very front row of folding chairs
that have been spread out all over the center of the shop and I
persuade her to compromise. Two rows back and to the side we
take our places and she looks around the store until her eyes land
on the man of the hour. "There he is!" She elbows me sharply in
the side. "At least he's smiling this time!"

I follow her gaze. It's true, this is the Aloysius Hunt I
recognize from his author photograph. His thinning hair is
neatly styled and there's something suspiciously smooth and
even about his skin tone that suggests makeup, but he looks a lot

more cheerful than when we first saw him. He nods and smiles as he talks to two other people I'm only vaguely familiar with.

"Who's he talking to?" Cassie is nothing if not curious.

"Well, that's the principal of Silver Brook High School," I say, pointing to the gentleman of the pair, whose double-denim look screams *trying hard to look casual* and is entirely at odds with his straight spine and square shoulders. "Oh, look! There's a couple of students with him." I wave at three teenagers beyond him, recognizing one, Jessica, from our stint as elves at Santa's grotto last Christmas. She immediately ditches her two friends and comes over to say hello.

"What are you doing here?" I frown as she flops down into the chairs in front of us. "I didn't take you for a murder mystery fan."

"I'm not." She rolls her eyes. "But I'm working on a true-crime podcast with Kalen and Anthony for extra credit. And it gets us out of school early for the day." She notices Cassie for the first time and shrinks into herself, shy.

"This is my aunt." I hurry to introduce them, and Cassie beams at her new friend.

"Jessica, is it? What a pretty name. I knew a Jessica once...or was it Jennifer...?"

"I think you're being summoned." I nod towards Principal Dexter, who's trying to attract Jessica's attention and she shoots Cassie and me a mischievous smile before hurrying off to join her friends.

"Mr Hunt certainly looks a lot happier than when we saw him earlier on today," Cassie comments, as the door opens and the rest of the gathered fans start to make their way into the shop. I hear the Superfans before I see them and fight a laugh as they descend en-masse, occupying the row of seats directly in front of Cassie and me.

"I'm surprised he's so relaxed," I say, reminded of something by the people in front of me. "If he's been getting death threats."

Cassie's eyebrows rise and I point to the Superfans chattering excitedly in front of us, indicating where I got this latest piece of information from.

"I suppose there's nowhere safer than to be surrounded by a crowd of supporters," she says, with a faint frown as she fixes her eyes on Hunt. "He certainly seems to attract plenty of those."

I follow her gaze and roll my eyes. Bernadette Peterson, Silver Brook's dedicated librarian, looks like the living embodiment of a heart-eyes emoji. She's dressed in black from head to foot, like usual, but instead of scowling at the people who dare to cross the threshold of the tiny, tumble-down library building to disturb her books and disrupt her peace and quiet, she's hanging off every smug word Aloysius Hunt chooses to share. She's clutching a well-worn paperback of one of his earlier works, eager for him to endorse it with his signature.

"That's about the happiest I've ever seen Bernie," I mutter to my aunt, who catches my eye with a wry smile. "I'm kind of surprised she isn't trying to persuade him to accompany her back to the library for an author event of her own." I fight a laugh. "Mind you, that would mean encouraging people into the library instead of away from it."

"Isn't that the point of a public library?" Cassie asks me. "That the public have access to it?"

"Oh, we have access," I reassure her. "Bernie just resents us for it. She'd much rather we all came to Peter for our reading needs instead of messing up her nice, neat shelves." I tilt my head to one side, picturing something I'd never thought of before. "They're kind of the perfect couple..."

"The author and the librarian?"

I burst out laughing, so much that both Bernie and Mr Hunt turn to look at us and I hurry to bury my head in my purse, rummaging away until I have control over myself again.

"Stop trying to matchmake everyone you meet," I tell my aunt when I surface, checking my phone for any messages. My thumb strays over to Rob's name but there's been nothing since his *have a nice day* message this morning, and I look at that a moment too long.

"Don't be bitter, Meredith." Cassie's eyes twinkle. "Just because you've taken yourself off the market doesn't mean other people aren't looking." She lifts her hand and waves across the room at someone who's caught her eye and for a moment I think her earlier conquest has followed us here. No, she's waving at Peter Stalker, who blushes and turns his head as soon as he sees me looking. *Ew*.

"There's looking and there's *looking*," I tell her, with a pointed glare. "And I thought you came all this way to see me, not find yourself a new boyfriend."

"I did." She winks at me. "But who says I can't multitask?"

Aloysius Hunt's voice drifts towards us and I find myself tuning into the self-satisfied drone. Bernie is still hanging off every word he says, and she's been joined in her circle of admiration by two of the women I recognize from the group of Superfans. Even Principal Dexter is lingering a little too long and smiling a little too widely. I'm all for a little celebrity-worship but this is starting to get a bit ridiculous.

There's something about the smug smile Hunt is wearing, the way his eyes flutter closed as if he can't bear his own brilliance that makes my stomach turn over. Until this moment I'd quite liked Aloysius Hunt, but the two times I've seen him today have swiftly shattered my earlier opinion of him. My gaze slides along to the pile of hardback books stacked artistically on a table in front of us and I wonder if my love affair with this particular brand of murder mystery is about to come to a crashing halt now I've glimpsed the man behind them.

"They say this is quite a deviation from his previous work." One of the Superfans - Eleanor, I think her name is - is deep in discussion with her friends and I find myself curiously listening in. Despite Cassie and me eagerly trading every one of Aloysius Hunt's previous books, neither of us has snagged a copy of his latest mystery novel.

"It'll be a work of genius, as far as I'm concerned. I never can work out whodunnit!" Eleanor's companion says with an adoring sigh. "He's so smart!"

Cassie pointedly clears her throat beside me and I glance at her, willing her not to barge into a conversation between strangers. Neither one of us thinks very highly of Aloysius Hunt after the behavior he's exhibited so far today, but I'm holding out hope things will improve this afternoon. *After all*, I reason. *It must be nerve-wracking to debut a new book. Especially if you've been dealing with death threats...* I shiver as I recall what I heard earlier in the cafe and wonder just how it is Hunt is managing to laugh and flirt and be apparently cheerful when he was so bad-tempered earlier. *I suppose it helps when you're talking to someone who admires you, not someone who works for you.* I catch sight of the young man from earlier, standing next to the young woman who'd been with him. He looks pale and agitated and keeps checking his watch, which makes me think he's eager for the book launch to begin. *Or to get it over and done with.*

"Patrick!" Hunt straightens, looking around for somebody. "Patrick!"

The young man jumps to attention, shaking off his girlfriend's hold and striding towards his boss.

"You forgot one of the boxes of books. Look at this! It throws the whole symmetry of the design off."

Patrick frowns, glancing from the table to Mr Hunt and back again.

"Well?"

There's a crack of thunder overhead which makes the whole audience jump, and Patrick wearily pulls his shirt collar up against the weather outside.

"I'll go now," he says, accepting the car keys Hunt holds out to him.

"Take my jacket," the author says, shrugging out of his long trench-coat. It dwarfs the younger man, but he wears it gratefully, eyeing the dark clouds outside.

"I'll come!" The girl takes a step forwards but both men shake their heads and she reluctantly stays put, shooting an irritated glance at Hunt, who turns back to his adoring crowd of admirers. I see Peter Stalker trying to edge his way into the conversation but at the sound of the words *public library* he steps back, exchanging a glare with Principal Dexter, who has been pulled into conversation with his podcast team, discussing where and how to set up their equipment.

"Well, I'm glad we rushed to get here," Cassie whispers to me, in a tone of voice that makes it hard to tell whether she's joking or not. She winks. "It's amazing how many tiny dramas are unfolding around us all the time if only we can be bothered to notice!"

Chapter Four

"Well, Mr Hunt, we're really pleased you've agreed to join us on our true-crime podcast, Sleuthing Silver Brook!" Jessica pauses before giving an exaggerated nod to Anthony, who fumbles with his sound set up and blasts a loud, menacing jingle that makes the audience wince until he hastily lowers the volume.

"Sorry," he mutters.

"*Mr. Hunt!*" Jessica yells, as the jingle abruptly stops. She clears her throat and tries again. "Mr. Hunt. You're a mystery writer and you're here in town to launch your new book, is that right?"

"That's right, Jessica." Hunt beams at the crowd and gets an appreciative ripple of applause in return. "Although I'm not sure how much I can tell you about *true* crime, ho ho. It's a dangerous business, writing, but I'd like to assure you all the murder and mayhem in my novels is strictly fictional." The applause gives way to collective laughter and Hunt offers a few warm anecdotes about his writing career to date. "Of course," he continues. "I'm no stranger to Silver Brook. I grew up here, did you know that?"

I look at Cassie, who is as surprised by this revelation as I am. The little group of Superfans in front of us seem entirely unfazed by this, so I guess it's not exactly a secret.

"That's right," Hunt says. "In fact, I was a student at your very own high school! Poor old Principal Dexter is still rather put out that I chose to launch my book here, in Peter Stalker's Bookstore, and not at the high school with all of you."

I glance at the principal who's standing a few feet away, observing his students from a distance, and see his features slide into a scowl. He looks more than a little put out. But in another moment, Hunt's made some kind of a joke that makes everyone laugh again, including Principal Dexter, so I tell myself I'm imagining things. *Just because Aloysius Hunt writes about death and disaster doesn't mean he stirs it up everywhere he goes.*

"She's good, isn't she?" Cassie leans over and whispers in my ear. "Jessica. She'd make an excellent reporter one day!"

"I guess." My cheeks flush guiltily as I realize I've been so distracted by a potential spat between Aloysius Hunt and Principal Dexter that I've barely paid any attention to Jessica's interview. I fix my gaze on her, determined to offer some solid praise for her performance.

"Well, Mr. Hunt, on behalf of all the students at Silver Brook High, I'd like to thank you for taking the time to talk with us today. And we'll be back next week for another unmissable episode of Sleuthing Silver Brook. Hope you'll join us then!" Jessica freezes, and a ripple of awkward silence makes its way around the room until Anthony clears his throat.

"Uh, that's it. I'll add the jingle in later." He nods. "In editing." There's a giggle or two from the audience and then everyone bursts into applause, wanting to cheer this small group of teenagers on a job well done.

"Fabulous work, everyone. Just fabulous!" Peter Stalker strides into the front of the room, laying a companionable arm around Hunt's shoulders. "We'll break for some refreshments, shall we? Then we can get down to the real reason we're all here today. Mr. Hunt, allow me..."

There's a momentary chaos of people moving around, climbing over chairs and talking with one another and I see my cupcakes laid out on a table on one side of the room. I sigh. They aren't arranged in any way that you might call artistic, but that's on Peter, not me, and I'm pleased to see them eagerly being snapped up by the milling crowd of hungry readers.

"Well, I'm going to try and get my book signed right away!" Eleanor declares as she jumps up from her chair. "I bought the very first Aloysius Hunt novel I ever read - and I'm going to ask him to sign it. That'll be so much more personal than just picking up his latest book like everybody else..."

Two of her friends follow her, and I draw in a breath, wondering if Mr Hunt is quite ready to be ambushed by adoring fans before he's even properly launched his newest book.

"Do you want a cupcake, Merry?" Cassie asks me. Before I even have time to turn my head she's hopped up and disappeared into the crowd, but I notice she bypasses the snack table altogether, making straight for the bent blonde head of the young woman we saw earlier. A moment later, Cassie escorts her back to join me, and I move down a chair to make some space for the new arrival.

"This is Phoebe Simms. She's here with her boyfriend - Mr Hunt's assistant." She shoots me a significant look and I smile, urging Phoebe to take a seat.

"Mr Hunt's assistant. That must be a very interesting job."

"You'd think so." Phoebe looks down at her phone, taps out a message, then lifts her head. "I suppose it was, to begin with, but lately..."

I remember the angry exchange between the two men we witnessed earlier today on the street and wonder what Aloysius

Hunt is really like when he isn't on his best behavior before a crowd of adoring fans.

"And what about you, Phoebe?" Cassie prompts. "Are you an aspiring writer too?"

She shakes her head vehemently and I notice the scowl she's wearing as she looks at the poster advertising Hunt's newest release.

"I'm only here to keep Patrick company. But he -" She looks down at her phone again, and when her head lifts now I think I see tears in her eyes.

"Your young man has been gone quite a while," Cassie agrees, consulting her watch. "He went to fetch another box of books, didn't he?"

"From the back of the car." Phoebe nods, and as another crash of thunder sounds overhead we all flinch. "He'll be absolutely soaked by now." She bites her lip. "And so will the books."

"I'll go and look for him," Cassie announces, never one to let an opportunity to stick her nose in go untaken. "Tell me where he parked."

"I'll go," I say, grabbing my aunt by the arm and encouraging her to stay put. "You're new in town, remember? At least I stand a chance of finding my way there and back." I smile at Phoebe. "Don't worry. I'm sure everything's fine. You'll be in the parking bay behind the shop, right?"

I've barely finished speaking when the door to Peter Stalker's bookshop flies open and a man stands there, a flash of lightning illuminating the panic in his features.

"Mr Hunt? Mr Aloysius Hunt? Come quickly - there's been a dreadful accident!"

• • • •

DESPITE THE RAIN, ALMOST everyone follows the man outside, a crowd of people craning their necks to see what has happened. Mr Hunt along with Peter, Principal Dexter, and a few others make their way to the front of the crowd and that's when Phoebe breaks free of me and Cassie and bolts after them. She lets out a bloodcurdling scream and Cassie looks at me before we, too, break formation and rush to support our new friend.

"It's Patrick!" she sobs, pointing at what has already captured the attention of everyone else around us. A familiar-looking vintage car has rolled down the slope of the narrow parking area, crushing someone between its back bumper and the bookstore's exterior wall.

"I can't move him! Can't move the car, either." The first man who came to alert us to the tragedy is walking around the scene, shaking his head in despair. "I think - I think he's dead."

"Well, somebody call for an ambulance!" Cassie says, sharply. "Or get the police here. Somebody should be able to do something!"

She looks for a moment like she's going to stride forward and try her own strength at sliding the car away from the poor trapped body, but before she can there's the wail of a siren and an ambulance swerves down the sodden street towards us, coming to an abrupt halt before two EMT's scramble out.

"Come on, honey," Cassie says, patting Phoebe warmly on the shoulder. "We shouldn't stand here watching this."

"Quite so...ah...yes. Quite so." Peter Stalker looks a little green around the gills but he seems to remember he's technically in charge of the assembled crowd and tries to herd us all back towards the bookstore. I exchange a look with my aunt and we carefully extricate ourselves from the crowd, making a swift retreat to the Jitterbug Junction where we can have some peace and quiet.

Phoebe doesn't object which surprises me but when I catch a glimpse of the distant look in her eyes I figure she's not really aware of what's happening, or where we're taking her.

"We'll make a nice pot of tea, that's what we'll do first of all." Aunt Cassie is speaking in a low voice, and I wonder if it's for our benefit or hers. I find myself tuning into her soft, comforting tones. "A nice cup of tea for all of us and maybe a little something sweet. That's always good after a shock. And then me or Merry will find out what's going on."

"I should wait with - with him." Phoebe stops rigidly and tries to turn back but neither me nor my aunt are going to let her.

"Let the EMTs do their job, dear," Cassie says, gently. "Let's get out of this rain and then we'll decide what to do next."

Phoebe nods, obedient as a child, and soon we reach the cafe which is still deserted. I leave the sign turned to *closed* and don't bother putting any extra lights on. The last thing I want to do is encourage customers, although between the weather and the parking area catastrophe I don't imagine there'll be many of them.

I slowly make us all something to drink and we sit in a sort of stupor for what might be minutes or hours, I can't tell, but all of a sudden the door to the cafe bursts open and I am fully prepared to chase off customers I can ill-afford to lose when I recognize the tall, balding figure of Police Chief Trainor.

"Merry! Excellent, I hoped I'd find you here. Why don't you brew us up some coffee, and I can take your statements while I'm waiting." He glances around the cafe, looking a little disappointment to find only three of us in there. "Where is everybody?"

"Everybody?" I ask, knowing exactly who he is looking for.

"Aloysius Hunt!" he booms. "The intended victim of the murder!"

"Murder?" Cassie clutches hold of Phoebe, who has been stunned out of her sobs. "Surely not! It was an accident, wasn't it? And that poor young man..."

"Crushed. It's a horrible thing." There's an unfortunately cheery ring to Trainor's voice and I cringe, wishing that it was my best friend and police officer, Kate Kelly, and not the police chief delivering this news. She at least might have used a little tact.

"I think Mr. Hunt stayed at the book shop," I say, hurrying over with a very full cup of coffee I thrust into the police chief's hand. "In fact, I think everyone went back there. Nobody wanted to wait around in the rain, and with the EMT's there..."

"Quite, quite." He takes a scalding sip and shakes his head at me. "Bad business. Very tragic. And quite clearly a case of the wrong person in the wrong place at the wrong time." He shivers. "It's obvious the murderer meant to kill Hunt."

"How so?" Cassie has left Phoebe's side and drifted towards us. She's eyeing the police chief in that very particular *explain yourself* look that I remember from my childhood, whenever I tried to sneak a lie past my all-knowing aunt's disbelieving eyes.

"Eh? What's that?"

"How is it obvious that the killer meant to kill somebody else? How is it obvious there was any killer at all? Surely it was a terrible, tragic accident."

"Nope." Trainor shakes his head, taking another sip of his coffee before delivering the news. "The brakes were sheared through. It was parked on a slope. As soon as anything moved in that car it was destined to roll back and crush whoever stood in the way. I think you'll agree, we're looking at a murder."

Chapter Five

The rain stops falling sometime in the afternoon, but the whole of Silver Brook still feels like it's under a big black cloud. Cassie and I half-heartedly open up the cafe again, but everyone who comes in wants to discuss the latest drama unfolding in our small, sleepy town. Everyone has a theory about the death on the high street, and every mention of Aloysius Hunt or his poor assistant sends Phoebe into fits of tears. After what feels like hours, my friend Kate - or I suppose I should stick with *Officer Kelly* as she's here in an official capacity - calls in and I point out Phoebe, who is sitting silently at a corner table while my Aunt Cassie tries to draw her into completing a crossword puzzle.

"Is there any news?" I ask my friend, as I fix her regular drink. "How's the investigation going?"

"Strangely!" Kate frowns and glances down at her phone. "At first it didn't seem like there was going to be one. It was just a tragic accident. Then someone spotted the brake cables were cut-deliberately cut, I mean - and that made the accident theory a whole lot less convincing." She taps her phone a few times and then slides it into her pocket. "And of course, there's the death threats."

"Oh yeah! I heard about those!"

Kate's eyes narrow and I start feeling like I'm the one under interrogation.

"From Hunt's roaming pack of Superfans." I point to the group, most of whom have taken up residence in the same booth they occupied earlier, although everyone is a lot more subdued than they were before. "It seems to be fairly common knowledge that he had a stalker."

"Or several." Kate raises her eyebrows and accepts the cup I offer her with a grateful smile. "But thanks for letting me know. I'll add them to my list of people to interview."

"Anything I can do to help!"

Kate gives me a hard stare and my heart starts to beat a little more quickly.

"What?"

"Just...don't get too involved in this one, ok, Merry?"

"Define *too involved*?" I ask, with a nervous laugh. I know I'm developing something of a habit of being in the wrong place at the wrong time where murders are concerned, but at least this time I wasn't the one to find the body. My gaze strays to Phoebe without me meaning it to, and I see her head bent low in an intense conversation with Aunt Cassie. I bite my lip. If Cassie has taken Phoebe under her wing I guess there's no chance of me not being involved in this. *Not to mention the fact that if someone is running around Silver Brook killing off visitors, I want to know about it!* Cassie seems to feel my eyes on her because she looks up and waves at me, which makes Phoebe turn her head too. There's something in her eyes, a shadow that flickers across her face so quickly I'm not even totally sure I really see it. *Poor kid*, I think to myself, even though I'm probably only a few years older than she is. *I don't suppose she imagined losing her boyfriend like that.*

"Ok. Well, I think I'll go and have a word with Phoebe first if you don't mind. I want to find out a little more about Patrick." She winces. "And who might have wanted to hurt him."

"I thought you were looking at Aloysius Hunt as the potential victim. Wasn't he the one getting the death threats?"

"He was." Kate frowns. "But he wasn't the one who ended up dead, now, was he?"

I nod, considering this. Chief Trainor was convinced from the get-go that this attack had been meant for Hunt all along - that Patrick was just in the wrong place at the wrong time.

"He was wearing Hunt's jacket," I remember, and Kate turns to look at me. "Patrick was. He borrowed it because of the rain."

She nods slowly.

"I suppose in the shadows, and with his hood pulled up..."

"And it was Hunt's car. A four-door convertible. It's sort of his trademark." I offer a thin smile. "One of them."

"Thanks, Merry." Kate's expression shifts into neutral and I can see her move into police-officer mode. She's grateful for my input, but now it's time for her to do her job.

And time for me to do mine, I think, looking up as the cafe door swings open and another damp customer scurries indoors, eager for coffee and a news update. I'm startled to recognize Principal Dexter shaking out his umbrella as he steps into the cafe without his student entourage.

"Double espresso," he barks as he strides up to the counter to pay. "To take away."

"Did you get the kids home ok?" He frowns as he looks at me, then realizes I was at the bookstore just the same as he was. He nods, vaguely, but keeps his gaze fixed on the card machine, ready for it to flash into life.

"Has there been any news?" he asks, as I make up his order and hand it over to him. "It's such a tragedy."

"Yes." My gaze travels without me meaning it to and Principal Dexter follows it, seeing Kate's head bent low as she talks to Phoebe and my aunt.

"Isn't that the girlfriend?"

I nod.

"Such a tragedy," Principal Dexter says again. "But I suppose the grim reaper is coming for all of us sooner or later." He takes a scalding sip of his coffee. "Mind you, this never would have happened if Hunt had done the launch at the high school like I suggested. We have a huge parking lot, nice and flat. No chance of anyone having any accidents there."

I glare at him but he doesn't seem to think there's anything wrong with his comment.

"I wonder if I can persuade him to swing by the school tomorrow..."

"You'll have to ask him," I say, icily. "I expect the police will want everyone to stay in town so it's not like he'll be going anywhere. What with the murder investigation going on."

"Murder?" Principal Dexter lets out a choked little laugh, then sets down his coffee and stares at me. "Did you say murder?"

I nod and feel a tiny glint of satisfaction as the color drains out of his face.

"It looks like it wasn't just an accident of parking after all. Someone meant for somebody to die today, and they were determined to use Aloysius Hunt's car as the murder weapon. So I guess it's a good job they didn't do it at the high school, otherwise you'd be at the center of a scandal, Principal Dexter."

He visibly shudders, then takes his coffee and his umbrella and hurries out into the storm. I shake my head slowly, wondering what it is about Aloysius Hunt that makes the people around him so keen to have him all to themselves. One of the Superfans waves frantically in my direction and I saunter towards them, ready to take another round of drinks orders and wondering how long it'll be before I can shut up shop and go home. I'm exhausted and ready to kick my heels up and snuggle with my cat and do nothing for a while.

"We were talking, Merry, and were hoping you could help us settle an argument."

"Oh?" I look warily at their table, which is completely covered with sheets of notepaper, pens, and paperback books. I reach for one that looks familiar then snatch my hand back. It is familiar - I've had it sitting on my nightstand for the last week. *Death by Driving*. The title takes on a whole new sinister meaning for me now, and I realize why there's been a nagging sense of deja vu about everything that's happened so far today.

"Yes!" Eleanor crows, lifting the book and thrusting it towards me. "You see it too, don't you? I knew you would be on the same wavelength as us."

"Some of us." Eleanor's friend interrupts and earns herself a filthy look from the unofficial leader of the group.

"Most of us," Eleanor concedes. She turns to me. "Have you read this one? It just struck me this afternoon, after - well, after that dreadful business at the bookstore." She pauses and the Superfans take a moment of awkward silence.

"What about it?" I ask, uncertainly.

"Well, the manner of death. The brakes being cut on the car. A person being crushed to death." She waves the book at me. "It's exactly what happened in here! Deaths one and two." She frowns. "Of course, I guess they didn't both happen at once."

"Exactly!" Eleanor's dissenting friend is triumphant. "And the cut brakes didn't lead to a death, just an injury." She looks at me. "Fenella Inglethorpe ends up with a broken leg, remember?"

I nod, although it's a while since I read this particular murder mystery. I do remember the crush injury though, and the way it had been believed to be an accident for the middle third of the book.

"Can I borrow this?" I take it without asking and drift over to where Kate's sitting with Aunt Cassie and a finally dry-eyed Phoebe. She looks at me, frowning a little in concern.

"Are you alright, Merry? You look like you've seen a ghost."

"You need to look at this." I pass Kate the book. "Because I can't say for sure, but I think this might be what our killer used to plan his crime."

Chapter Six

B y the time it's finally time to close up and head home, I'm exhausted. Cassie's exhausted. And Phoebe...

"Phoebe's going to come and stay with us." Cassie still has her arm wrapped tightly around Phoebe's thin shoulders. "That's ok with you, isn't it? She's so upset, poor lamb. We just can't send her off to that wretched little inn all on her own!"

The Silver Brook police department has insisted everyone who was at the book launch stays in town overnight and has block-booked the Harmony Inn out, which will make its owner, Hannah Kincaid, very happy. She's always touting for business, and Silver Brook isn't exactly the tourist capital of America. *Nothing like a murder to put a place on the map*, I think with a shiver.

"The Harmony Inn is actually quite nice," I protest, wincing at the thought of Hannah Kincaid's third-generation bed-and-breakfast being called "wretched". I see Phoebe's eyes fill with yet more tears and quickly shoot her a reassuring smile. "But of course you can come and stay with us. It'll be fine."

"It'll be more than fine," Cassandra declares. "It'll be fun. You can sleep in my room, Phoebe, and I'll bunk in with you, Merry. It'll be like a real old-fashioned sleepover."

Right, I think, wondering if my aunt realizes that the traumatized *little lamb* she's bringing home for the night is not going to be in any frame of mind to do face masks and sing karaoke. *Just nobody mention the murder game...*

"Oh, there's one thing I should tell you," I say over my shoulder to Phoebe as we all climb out of the car and make our way towards my house. I fumble for my keys and unlock the door. "I have a cat."

Snuffy barely gives me time to finish speaking before he hurls himself out of the door and right at my knees, digging his claws in so that I yelp.

"Good evening, your highness," I mutter, yanking his little feet free and scooping him into my arms. "This is Aunt Cassie who I was telling you about, and this is our friend Phoebe. They're both going to be staying with us tonight. Do you think you can handle that?"

He burrows deeper into my arms and lets out a contented purr that I would happily argue is a *yes*.

"Come in," I call, pushing the door open and ushering my guests into the house. "Make yourselves at home."

Snuffy wriggles to be let down, and as soon as I drop him onto his feet, he scurries towards Cassie's open suitcase and is soon having a wonderful time romping around in her belongings.

"Snuffy!" I shriek, trying to pull him free, but Cassie only laughs.

"Let him alone!" She pats me on the arm. "There's nothing all that valuable in there." She turns to the suitcase. "Just try not to destroy all my clothes, ok, cat?" Snuffy makes another happy little chirrup and I mentally catalog what things I have in my wardrobe that would fit and flatter my aunt if desperate measures are called for. Then I look at Phoebe, thinking that whether or not Cassie's luggage gets ruined, our new friend doesn't even have any to begin with.

"I can find you a change of clothes, Phoebe, if you'd like," I say, leading her upstairs. "And you're welcome to have a hot shower before we get dinner ready."

"Thank you." She still looks a little dazed but there's a bit more colour in her cheeks and I think she's managed to go almost a whole hour without crying, so I'm starting to hope we might have turned a corner. Kitted out with a clean pair of pajamas and a fresh set of towels, I point Phoebe towards the bathroom and head back downstairs in time to see Snuffy curled up and purring happily on Aunt Cassie's lap as she stretches out on the sofa.

"You managed to salvage most of your belongings, then?" I ask, scratching the cat behind his ears as I sink down next to them on the sofa.

"Most of them. What a cutie this cat of yours is, Merry. I can see why you decided to take him in."

"He's not so bad," I say, smiling when Snuffy lifts his head and glares at me. I'm pretty sure he can speak English, and he certainly objects to anything he might consider an insult. I fish my phone out of my pocket and glance at it, surprised there's been no message from Rob. Mind you, I haven't texted him either. I fire off a quick *how's your day going* and let it lie, thinking I'll save filling him in on the latest Silver Brook goings-on until we can speak properly.

"So what did Kate say?" Cassie has dropped her voice to a whisper but she still takes a cursory glance overhead as if to reassure herself Phoebe is well and truly out of earshot. "Do they have any idea who is responsible for this?"

I shake my head and start to sift through all the information I've gleaned today.

"It sounds like poor Patrick was in the wrong place at the wrong time. The murderer evidently meant for harm to come to Mr. Hunt." Cassie tilts her head to one side and I start counting out my reasons. "He had at least one enemy amongst his collection of fans. Somebody was even sending him nasty letters including more than one death threat. And then Eleanor pointed out that the whole method was lifted straight out of one of his books."

"*Death by Driving*," Cassie nods. "I thought back over it when you showed Kate the book. I remember that one! It was such a fun mystery. So many deaths..." She trails off, turning a sickly green and I pat her gently on the arm.

"It was different from his usual books though, don't you think?" I frown, trying to remember. "The plot was convoluted and I enjoyed it, but it didn't much feel like an Aloysius Hunt book."

"I suppose all writers evolve over time," Cassie says, absentmindedly stroking Snuffy, who is snoring lightly, giving in to sleep at last. "And if he had help..."

"What do you mean?"

"Well, Phoebe was telling me about Patrick." We both look up as the shower switches off, and Cassie hurries through her words in a whisper. "He didn't start out as Hunt's assistant, he was a writer himself, and made Aloysius Hunt his mentor."

"Patrick was a writer too?"

Cassie nods, but we soon hear Phoebe's footsteps coming towards us and hastily change the subject.

"All better?" Cassie asks, and Phoebe nods, looking a lot more human than she did an hour ago. She flops down on an armchair opposite us and reaches for her bag, rummaging in the bottom of it for her phone. In the end, she has to unpack half of her belongings and my perpetually curious aunt can't help but comment on the pile of papers and bottles of ink Phoebe piles to one side.

"Ooh! Look at that calligraphy! I've always wanted to learn to write like that."

Phoebe flinches and reaches for the scraps of paper, shuffling them hastily out of sight.

"Maybe you could show me a little?" Cassie is nothing if not determined. "Later tonight, I mean. We could have a master-class!"

My phone starts to buzz in my pocket and I wriggle around to liberate it. I see Rob's face on the display and smile, before excusing myself to the kitchen to take the call. The relief I feel just seeing Rob again, even on a blocky, buffering facetime call, floods my body and it takes a bit of effort to look normal as I hit the answer button.

"Hi, Rob."

"Merry!" He freezes and I can see him frown. "What's wrong? You haven't stumbled over any more dead bodies without me, have you?" He's teasing me about the fact that our relationship is still pretty new but we've already been involved in not one but two murder cases together. My heart sinks and I'm silent for so long he quickly guesses the truth. "Ok, tel me everything." He draws a breath. "What happened?"

I try to explain about Patrick and the accident which was apparently not an accident, about Aloysius Hunt and his Superfans and his stalker. Rob lets out a low whistle.

"So we've brought Phoebe back to stay with us. She is - was - Patrick's girlfriend and she's distraught. Aunt Cassie is just focused on getting her through the night as well as we can." I sigh. "I don't know what we're going to do tomorrow."

"Well, Merry, I guess you're going to do what you've had a habit of doing since the first day I met you." Rob's voice is warm and I lean into it like the hug I so desperately want from him.

"What's that?"

"You're going to solve this murder."

Chapter Seven

I finish chatting to Rob, although he's not so keen to talk much about his conference now he knows I'm at the center of another murder investigation. Instead, I tell him more about Aloysius Hunt and all the strange goings-on surrounding him. He makes me promise to take care of myself before signing off and I feel a little better just having been able to share my thoughts with him. It's not like having him right here beside me, but it's better than nothing.

Phoebe and Cassie are chattering away in the other room and I pause to listen, hearing the words *penmanship* and *calligraphy* and decide to leave them to it. My aunt has always had a hundred different hobbies so I'm not at all surprised she wants to add calligraphy to the list. If Phoebe is happy to teach her a thing or two maybe that's a good thing for both of them. It'll certainly help to get Phoebe's mind off everything else that's happened today.

I make a start on dinner, opting for a simple lemon pasta dish, and soon have three steaming bowls to carry through to the other room.

"Look, Merry!" Cassie is bent over on the floor, tracing a careful sentence on a scrap of paper.

"Very nice," I say, even though I can hardly see what she's writing. Her head is only inches away from the paper and her gray hair blocks my view. "Do you want something to eat?"

Phoebe's ears prick up at this, and I take it as another good sign that she finally has her appetite back. She was a little waif-like to begin with and I'm determined to feed her up while she's under my roof. I pass her a bowl and set Cassie's down next to her, before retreating to the sofa. Snuffy glares at me and I remind him that his bowl of food is in the kitchen but he's much more interested in the parmesan in my pasta dish. I try to distract him while I eat and watch Phoebe and Cassie at work.

"You're picking it up really well," Phoebe says, looking admiringly at Cassie's calligraphy. "Very even. And you remembered what I said about the half-height and full-height letters."

"They certainly aren't anything compared to yours!" Cassie says, blushing a little all the same at this praise of her work.

"Mine?" Phoebe pauses with her fork halfway to her mouth. "What do you mean, mine?"

There's a strange sharpness to her voice and she's clasping her bowl so tightly that her fingertips have gone white. I wonder what's so shocking about my aunt's comment. Cassie rocks back in her seat and turns over the clutch of paper scraps she's been practicing on.

"Here!" She smiles. "I guess you made a mistake or something and didn't want to keep this, although it's so pretty it's a shame to see it torn into so many pieces."

Phoebe's face flushes red and she reaches for the papers but not fast enough. Cassie frowns, her lips moving as she reads the words Phoebe has discarded.

"Phoebe." Her voice takes on that same tone I remember from childhood whenever she caught me doing anything wrong. "What is this?"

I lean forward on the sofa, trying to see what's going on.

"It's nothing." Phoebe takes the papers out of Cassie's hands and crumples them into a ball. "Nothing important."

Both Cassie and I have gotten pretty good at spotting a liar when we need to, and Phoebe barely manages one more bite of her meal before her resolve weakens.

"It was just a letter," she admits, in a tiny voice. "One letter. Two. Three, tops. I just wanted him to think about what he was doing."

"Wanted who to think about what he was doing?" I ask, even though I think I already know the answer. My heart starts beating rapidly in my chest and I put down my pasta, barely noticing the interest Snuffy takes in it.

"Aloysius Hunt." Phoebe draws in a shaky breath. "I'm the person who sent him the threatening letters."

Silence descends on my living room like a blanket and Cassie and I stare at each other before looking back at Phoebe, who is tugging on a loose thread on her sleeve.

"It was just letters, though. That's it! I didn't - I wouldn't -" She starts to sob again but there's no tears left and in the end I go to her side, laying a comforting hand on her shoulder.

"Maybe you'd better tell us everything," I say. "Then we can figure out what to do next."

. . . .

"I NEVER MEANT TO ACTUALLY send them to him."

Phoebe is sitting at the head of the dining table in my cramped kitchen, with me on one side of her and Cassie opposite. She isn't looking at us, but she's spread the last few scraps of paper out in front of us, displaying only a few clear words. There's something incongruous about the cruel content and the elegant lettering, and I can only imagine how sinister it would have felt to receive something like this. It had taken time and patience to write these letters out by hand.

"It all started just as a way to vent my feelings. He was so unkind to Patrick." She sniffs but is determined to continue speaking now that she's started. "He didn't know anything about it. It was all me. But one weekend we'd been doing an event and Mr. Hunt was just so horrible. He'd promised to help Patrick with something he was writing but then he just claimed it had been so bad he hadn't been able to read more than a page. Patrick was crushed. And then he still had to go be on site as Hunt's assistant all day, listening to him encourage other writers and talking about his successes." She scowls. "He was so unkind, too, treating Patrick like dirt and reminding him that it was all thanks to Mr. Hunt that he was there to begin with."

"That must have been difficult to watch," I say, giving her hand an encouraging squeeze.

"It was." Phoebe nods. "And that night I'd just had enough. When we went back to our hotel, Patrick had to spend some more time with Mr. Hunt going over their schedule for the next day and I just went back to our room. I was bored so I pulled out my pens and ink and before I knew it, I was writing a letter." She shrugs her shoulders. "It felt good to finally get it out there on the page. But I wasn't going to send it. I should have thrown it away then and there, but I kept it. And then, two days later, he was just the same. Patrick was so upset but he wouldn't talk about it and I decided maybe it was time Aloysius Hunt knew what it was like to have someone say awful things to him for a change." She lifts her chin. "I slid the note under his hotel room door and even though he never talked about it I could tell it shook him up. He was nice to Patrick all the next day. Me too.

He used my actual name and everything." She smiles. "So then it became a sort of weapon. If he was particularly disagreeable he'd get a note, then he'd behave better for a little while." She shakes her head. "I never meant for anything else to happen." Her voice drops. "Especially not to - to Patrick."

Cassie looks at me, and I decide I'm going to have to be the one to say it.

"You know we can't just sit on this, Phoebe. We're going to have to tell someone. The police." Her head jerks up and I expect her to offer a list of excuses but to my surprise she nods and speaks in that same stiff, quiet voice.

"I know."

"And Mr. Hunt." Cassie leans across the table, taking Phoebe's other hand. "You need to tell him, too."

"Alright." Phoebe smiles and for the first time I realize she's a lot stronger than I've been giving her credit for. "Now that Patrick's gone, it's not like I ever need to see Aloysius Hunt again after this."

My eyes trace over the scraps of Phoebe's last, unsent letter but I can't help but feel a strange sense of disappointment. If she really is responsible for the threatening notes - and nothing else - that means we're nowhere closer to discovering who the real murderer is.

Chapter Eight

Early the next morning I send Aunt Cassie off to the police station with Phoebe in tow, leaving me to open up the Jitterbug Junction on my own. I've been doing it just about long enough that I have a system down, even though I know I'm going to need to hire some help sooner or later. I've made it through the first morning rush with minimal disasters when the door swings open and I see two familiar faces.

"What happened?" I ask, practically throwing my last customer's drink order at them, I'm so eager for news. I bustle out from behind the counter and drag Cassie and Phoebe to an empty table, forcing them to sit and tell me everything.

"There's not much to tell," Phoebe says, sliding a shoulder bag I don't recognize onto her lap and hugging it tightly.

"Kate took Phoebe's statement," Cassie says quickly. "Very nice about it she was, too. Let me sit in with her and wrote it all down." She shoots me a smile. "It doesn't make a great deal of difference to the investigation, but she's glad we came forward."

Phoebe lets out a loud, theatrical sigh and I turn to look at her, but Cassie is the one to provide an explanation.

"She also suggested we might like to explain it all to Aloysius Hunt. The letters. So that he knows he doesn't still have a crazed stalker sending him threatening notes everywhere he goes." She purses her lips. "So he isn't worried about danger coming from that quarter at least."

"Maybe you should have something to eat and drink first," I say, giving Phoebe an impromptu hug as I go back to the counter and plate up two apricot pastries and pour two lattes that I bring back to the table. Phoebe still looks very pale, and it's like she's retreated back into herself after her burst of honesty last night. I glance at Cassie, wondering if she's noticed, and the slightest pinch of a frown on her features suggests she has.

"Kate also gave us some of Patrick's belongings, didn't she?"

Phoebe hugs the battered shoulder bag a little closer, looking up at us defensively.

"I'm his next of kin," she protests. "Or near enough. He carried this bag with him everywhere." Her breath hitches. "And now it's all I have left of him."

"Not true," Cassie says sternly. "You have all your memories of him and the time you spent together. That's what you hold on to, dear. That's what will see you through rebuilding your life and moving on." Cassie knows what she's talking about. I've heard the story often enough of the first and only man she ever really loved - my Uncle Jack, who met and married Cassie after a whirlwind two-week romance. She was widowed within a year, and vowed never to marry again, and as far as I know, apart from a run of flings and flirtations, she's never even been tempted. Her voice wobbles just a little and I glance at her but when she sees my concern she smiles. "Now come on, Phoebe. Let's enjoy these tasty treats before we go and hunt down Mr Hunt." She notices her wordplay as she speaks and lets out a little squeak of laughter which lifts everybody's mood, and I'm pleased when Phoebe takes a small, mouse-like bite of her pastry.

The door swings open and admits a pair of women who are loudly arguing over something and my smile stretches thin when I recognize two of the Superfans making their way to the counter. Eleanor isn't leading the pack this time and I'm left scrambling for names I'm not sure I ever learned.

"Good morning, ladies!" I say brightly, as I slide back behind the register. "What can I get for you today?"

"Tea!" One of the ladies is wearing sunglasses despite the overcast day and she presses a hand theatrically against her temple. "Decaf, with lots of sugar. I have a dreadful headache. It's all the stress!"

"All the late night plotting you mean." Her companion is certainly light on compassion. She turns to me, her eyes bright and darting swiftly around as she looks to see who else is in the cafe this morning. "Isn't that -" She drops to a whisper. "The girlfriend?"

"Phoebe," I say, with a nod. "What would you like to drink, Ms. -?" I pause, inviting her to introduce herself but instead she clasps a hand to her heart and feigns sorrow.

"It's just so tragic. That poor, poor young man! To give his life for dear Aloysius! I mean, it's not like anybody would have wanted to kill him if they didn't think he was somebody else. Someone important. Mind you..." She frowns, and I'm about to burst a blood vessel trying to keep my smile in place. "They didn't exactly look alike, did they? He was so..." She waves her hand around which I think is designed to illustrate the fact that Patrick was very tall and thin. "And Mr Hunt is..." She moves her hands apart, conjuring up the stouter figure of the older author.

"It was raining," I say. "I don't suppose visibility was very good. And Patrick was wearing Mr. Hunt's raincoat." I pause. "And anyway, it sounds like the killer wasn't actually on the scene when the incident took place."

"They set it up ahead of time, June, I told you that last night." Ms. Sunglasses sounds irritable and I wonder how many times they've circled around this particular conversation in the last few hours.

"Well, then it was a bit of a risk if you ask me." June sniffs, annoyed that neither me nor her friend are eager to speculate any further. "Anyone could have ended up crushed underneath that car. How could the killer be sure they'd trap Aloysius?"

"They didn't," I remind her drily and start making Ms. Sunglasses' decaf tea while I wait for June to put in her order. "Poor Patrick ended up trapped instead."

"Exactly my point." June stares at me, wide-eyed, and I stare back, non-plussed. "Maybe it was meant to happen that way." She drops her voice to a whisper. "Maybe the killer wasn't going after Aloysius at all. Maybe they wanted to kill someone close to him as a warning. And the killer is still out there, so maybe poor, dear Aloysius is still in danger!" Her breath catches in the back of her throat as another, even worse idea occurs to her. "Maybe all of us are still in danger! We're all close to him. Any one of us could be next!" She looks dramatically around the crowded cafe and I bite my lip, fighting an urge to laugh. There's nothing comical about this, but the idea that these people could be in danger simply because they're fans of Hunts' work is ridiculous.

"She'll have the same as me," Ms. Sunglasses says, sliding them down her nose just long enough to give me a pointed look. "She certainly doesn't need any more caffeine today, do you, June?"

June gives a theatrical shiver and clutches her friend's arm.

"I won't feel easy until they figure out who's behind all this. First the letters, then the murder..." She shakes her head. "What next?"

"Some refreshments." Her friend shakes her off. "Oh, go and find us somewhere to sit, will you? You're so jumpy you're going to make me spill these drinks before we can even take a sip."

June obediently wanders off, idly circling the cafe until she finds an empty table and sits down at it, leaving her friend to pay for their order.

"Some people just can't help but put themselves at the very center of everything!" she says, with a sigh. "I love a good mystery as much as the next person, but I certainly don't think the whole of Smallbrook or whatever this town is called is in danger because one madman tried to murder an author."

I smile and decide this is not the time to point out how often Silver Brook has been rocked by cases just like this one lately.

Chapter Nine

"**A**re you sure you're happy leaving the Jitterbug, Merry?"

I nod, thinking of the *back in five minutes* sign I left taped over the front door, and hope it doesn't cost me too many loyal customers. I can't help it. I'm kind of curious to see Aloysius Hunt in the flesh and find out if he's as affected by what happened yesterday as Phoebe is. *And then there's Peter Stalker...*

To my surprise, the bookstore isn't empty. Not even close. It's busier than I've ever seen it. Busier than the Jitterbug during the daily lunch rush. There are people literally queueing out the door and there's nothing for me, Cassie, and Phoebe to do but join the line and wait for our turn to step inside.

"I've never seen so many people here!" I confess, staring at the eager readers. It's only as our spot in the queue moves closer to the door that I start to realize that Silver Brook hasn't been gripped with a sudden mania for reading. They're all here to see Aloysius Hunt - but not because he's launching a new book. Everyone wants to meet the crime writer who narrowly avoided becoming a murder victim in his own right.

"Good morning! Come in! Good to see you!" Peter is standing guard at the doorway, and his genial manner slips when he recognizes me and Cassie. "Meredith." He frowns. "What are you doing here?"

"Shopping," I say, snatching a paperback from the shelf nearest me without even looking at it. "For books."

"I didn't realize you had a passion for the secret history of Silver Brook." He raises his eyebrows in amusement and I shove the thick local-history tome back, blushing that my ruse was so quickly seen through.

"I'm glad to see business is doing well," I tell him, acknowledging the crowds. "You were so worried nobody would want to come after...what happened."

"Yes, it's the funniest thing," Peter says, stroking his chin. "You'd think finding a body in my bookstore would be the very thing to put off the shoppers but it seems to have had the opposite effect." He chuckles and I draw a breath.

"You know they didn't actually find a body in your store," I tell him. "The accident happened outside."

"Well, I know. But with Aloysius Hunt being the intended victim...and launching his book here when it happened." His eyes narrow as he latches onto my last words. "And it wasn't an accident. What happened was -"

"We were here yesterday," Cassie reminds him, in her most imperious tone. "We know what happened. We wanted to come back today and see Mr. Hunt if that's ok with you. And we wanted to keep poor Phoebe company."

Poor Phoebe steps forward and her presence is enough to make Peter straighten. He smiles again, but this time it's a watery, sympathetic offering, and he allows us into the shop without any further questions.

"What a weasel of a man," Cassie mutters, in a low voice. "Perfectly happy to profit off of what happened. Look! He's altered yesterday's promotional material already!"

I turn my head to where piles of Aloysius Hunt's new novel sit - much smaller piles than yesterday, suggesting Peter's been doing a roaring trade all day. Then I see the addition to the signage and my stomach turns over. *"First he cheats death, then he writes about it!"*

"Maybe this isn't such a good idea," I say, wanting to keep Phoebe from having to face this particular demon.

"No," she says, drawing in a shaky breath. "I want to do this. I need to." Her hand goes to Patrick's bag and she clutches it closer to herself like a talisman. We press forward to where Mr. Hunt sits at a table, meeting and greeting half of Silver Brook and signing anything anyone offers him.

"Who's next?" he asks, turning from his latest fan to us. "Good morning, ladies! I...oh!" He spots Phoebe. "My dear girl!"

"Mr. Hunt."

He shakes his head, blinking back a suspicious lack of tears, and Phoebe switches to informality.

"Aloysius."

"Phoebe. Dear, dear Phoebe. How are you holding up?"

"I'm fine." She squares her shoulders, then reaches into Patrick's bag, bringing out the scraps of her unsent letter that we pieced together last night.

"What's this?" Hunt's gaze fixes on the bag and his smile freezes. "What have you got there?"

"It's a letter," Phoebe says, turning a couple of the scraps towards him so that he can see the familiar curlicued writing. "One I wrote but didn't send."

"One you wrote?" Hunt laughs, but the sound soon turns to a choked cough. "One *you* wrote?"

Phoebe nods, then curls her fingers around the scraps, crumpling them into a ball.

"I'm very sorry if my notes made you think you were in danger. I never meant anything by them I just - I was angry. And Patrick - and you -"

A riot of emotions flickers across Hunt's face. For a moment I think he's going to lunge across the table at Phoebe, or at the very least scream at her. He holds absolutely still for what feels like an endless moment, and then at last his features relax.

"You were my poison pen pal?" He shakes his head. "Well, Phoebe! I never would have guessed that!" He swallows. "What a surprise!"

"I'm sorry," Phoebe says again, then shoves the crumpled scraps back into Patrick's bag. "I've already been to tell the police about it."

"The police?" Hunt's gaze flickers back to the bag. He's watching Phoebe very carefully. "What did you tell them?"

"That I wrote those letters." Phoebe counts out the ones she sent and where she delivered them on her fingers. "That's all of them, isn't it?"

"I believe so." Hunt's face is surprisingly pale and I wonder if this news is hitting him harder than he's willing to admit. "Well, I'm pleased to know who was behind that little hate campaign. It doesn't negate the fact that someone - a murderer -"

"I was wondering, Mr. Hunt," I ask. The slightest flicker of one eyelid suggests that he's heard me, but he's still staring at Phoebe's bag. "Are you quite sure you're safe here in town? I mean, if somebody really did try to target you and failed, then there's every reason to suspect they might try again."

"Meredith! Ms Gray!"

I can hear Peter trying to attract my attention and ignore him. Sure, he might be mad that I'm trying to persuade his biggest attraction to leave town but it's for his own good. One murder might be good for the bookstore business, but two?

"Ah, you don't need to worry about that." Mr Hunt glances at me, the smug smile back on his face. He points and I see Police Chief Trainor propping up a wall in the corner of the store, idly watching the crowds of customers when he isn't looking at his phone. "I have my own police protection, whether I need it or not." He winks and I feel a little of my concern ebb away. That's something, I guess. I slide my arm around Phoebe and we turn away from the table, but before we can move more than a step or two, Hunt clears his throat and calls after us. "Phoebe? Phoebe, dear..."

We stop and all three of us turn back.

"Where - where did you get that bag?"

For the first time since I saw him yesterday, Aloysius Hunt seems unsettled. He's almost shaking and I wonder what is so upsetting about seeing Patrick's belongings in the possession of his girlfriend.

"That's Patrick's bag, isn't it?" he asks, running a hand through his thinning hair. "I remember he was never without it. He kept all manner of things in it, and I wonder - I mean, surely he'd like me to -"

"The police said I could have it," Phoebe says, dumbly.

"Well, yes. Of course. Yes." Hunt frowns. "But if you happen to look inside it, if you find -"

"There's just some old notebooks," Phoebe says, rummaging in the bag and lifting out a weatherbeaten spiral book. She flips the pages, but all it shows is a chaos of scribbling, crossings-out and underlining. "Just notes and things from all of our trips."

"I should look through them," Hunt says, reaching for the books. "I certainly wouldn't want to trouble you with -"

"I want to keep them." Phoebe can be just as stubborn as her boss when she wants to be it seems, and right now she wants to be. "They were the last things Patrick touched, before - before -" She sucks in air and both Cassie and I can see another torrent of tears is coming soon.

"Come on, dear," Cassie says. "Let's go back to the cafe. We've done all we needed to here."

"Yes, yes," Hunt says, looking grave. "Quite so. I'll see you soon, Phoebe. You take care."

Chapter Ten

I almost feel a little deflated at the lack of eager customers queueing outside of the Jitterbug Junction when Cassie, Phoebe, and I get back there. *You need a dead body of your own!* That cheery, black-comedy thought comes courtesy of my friend Jeremy, and I can just picture what his face would be if he said it. Jeremy has been out of town for a couple of weeks now caring for a sick family member. I feel a glimmer of satisfaction at how disappointed he's going to be to miss this latest Silver Brook drama, even though he won't regret not being caught up in it like he was the last time we had a murder to solve.

A murder to solve. That's what Rob had said to me about all this, and now I wonder if we'll ever get to the bottom of who killed Patrick. Phoebe seems to have just about come to terms with the fact that he's gone, although I don't imagine she will keep working with Aloysius Hunt for long. I wonder what she'll do when all this blows over.

"Phoebe," I ask, as I slide the *Back in five minutes* sign off the front door and await the inevitable - but apparently delayed - deluge of hungry coffee fans.

"Yes?" She's still clutching Patrick's bag like it's a lifeline and I review my earlier opinion. It's still so raw that it'll take a while before Phoebe is able to think about the future.

"Is there anyone we can call for you? Mom and Dad? Sister? Friend?" I glance at Cassie, who nods encouragingly, sensing that this is a good idea of mine. "You're going to need some support now - now that Patrick's gone."

"He's all I had," she says, sadly. "And I was all he had. Well, just me and Mr. Hunt. And his books."

I nod, thinking back over how often a stack of good books to read has helped me through a hard time. I don't suppose murder mysteries are going to offer any kind of comfort to Phoebe just now, but maybe something else. Cassie has the same idea.

"Maybe we should take a wander down to the library, dear. See if we can't find something nice to read. Or a recipe book. Maybe you and I can make dinner for Merry tonight."

I smile, then remember just how bad Aunt Cassie is at cooking.

"I don't mind cooking!" I say. "Or we could get takeaway..." Their heads are bent together, conspiring, and I see movement out of the corner of my eye that turns out to be a much-needed customer, coming for an afternoon pick-me-up.

"Eleanor!" I smile, pleased to see my favorite of the Superfans. Only this time, she's alone. "Where are your friends?"

"Heading out of town." She frowns. "They are such a bunch of quitters. They've decided this crime is unsolvable so they're all going back to their real lives."

"And you're sticking around?"

"I'm waiting until we know for sure Aloysius is safe!" There's something so intense about her that I feel a little intimidated myself, even though I've done nothing wrong. "He's had all those dreadful letters, after all! Who knows when the poison pen killer will strike again?"

"Ah..." I peer over Eleanor's shoulder to where Phoebe is standing next to my aunt and wonder whether she wants her nasty-note-writing-past shared beyond the few of us who already know all about it. "I think the police have decided there's no link between the letters and the murder," I say. "And I know for a fact they are keeping a very close eye on Mr Hunt."

"Well, that's not particularly reassuring." Eleanor's frown lifts a tiny bit and I wonder if she shares my opinion of Silver Brook's poor excuse for a police chief. Then I remember his second in command is my best friend Kate and brighten.

"Trust me," I tell her, whipping up a vanilla latte before she even has to ask for one. "The truth will come out in the end. Murderers tend to get found out before too long. They get cocky, they make a mistake, they -"

"Try again..."

"Yes." I'm watching Phoebe, the way she clutches the bag that was Patrick's, and a thought slowly dawns on me. *Most murderers only try again if they need to cover their tracks. They're taking out a threat - removing someone who can incriminate them. Or if they killed the wrong person to begin with.* I blink, my mind worrying at the thought like it's picking at a scab. *But what if this murderer had the right person all along? What if they never meant to kill Aloysius Hunt? What if Patrick was the intended victim?*

· · · ·

I DON'T HAVE TIME TO do much more than consider this idea for a few minutes before I'm caught up in the regular onslaught of customers and I am so busy that for a while I don't have time to think about anything at all. When I at last get a break long enough to look around for a few minutes I see Phoebe and Cassie's heads are bent over their table and I half expect to find them working on a new calligraphy lesson. I'm pleased to find that Phoebe has kept onto that hobby, even if she's letting go of the nasty notes she wrote using it. I frown and decide to take a closer look. I hope she's let go of the nasty notes...

"Look! This is it! Word for word!"

I'm startled to discover that Phoebe and Cassie aren't sitting alone. Eleanor has joined them, and all three of them are hard at work on a project that has nothing to do with calligraphy.

"What's going on?" I ask, keeping my tone light as I drift a little closer.

"We have discovered something, Merry!" Cassie waves a paperback book at me and it's not until I come a little closer that I recognize it. *Death by Driving* - it's the same book that Eleanor first flagged to me as having a lot in common with the way poor Patrick lost his life.

"What?" I ask, bracing for more gory details. Does my aunt have a detailed knowledge of automobile sabotage? Honestly, it wouldn't surprise me.

"Aloysius Hunt didn't write this book." Eleanor's the one who blurts out this information and I'm so surprised it takes me a minute to react.

"It's true, Merry! We have proof!" Cassie picks up a pile of loose-leaf, printed papers and I'm so mystified I lift one to my eyes for a closer look. "Page seventy-eight," Cassie hisses to Eleanor, who flips pages until she comes to that one, then clears her throat and starts to read.

"Major Archibald Darcy had always considered his Rolls Royce Phantom his most prized possession. It was the first thing he thought of when he woke up in the morning and the last thing he thought of when he closed his eyes at night..."

She looks up at me, all expectation, and I let out a bemused laugh.

"That's what it says here, word for word." My eyes slide from Eleanor to Cassie, to Phoebe. "And?"

"We found them folded in the back of one of Patrick's notebooks," Cassie says. "Excerpts - near enough the whole book. Only one or two little changes but certainly not enough to make them anything other than nearly identical."

I'm still not getting it and in the end, Phoebe is the one to explain.

"Aloysius Hunt didn't write these pages," she says calmly, sliding a few more of them out of the bag she's now clinging to like it's a life buoy. "Patrick did."

Chapter Eleven

"And we're sure Patrick wasn't just holding onto these pages for his boss?" I ask, for what feels like the hundredth time. "Maybe he had been editing them."

"Show her." Cassie can be quite bossy at times - it's a family trait that I certainly never exhibit - but in this instance it's put to good use. "Phoebe. Show her."

Phoebe reluctantly reaches back into the bag and pulls out one last sheet of paper, folded into a small square. She glances at me, all hesitation, then hands it over. Everyone is staring at me in suspense and I hurriedly unfold the page and look at it, my skin crawling as I make sense of the few typed lines.

Acknowledgments. To my mentor and friend, Aloysius Hunt, for all the advice and assistance he gave after a lifetime of writing mystery fiction to a brand new writer just starting out. I never could have done this without you. And to Phoebe, the love of my life, for always believing in me. This is book one of many, and I dedicate them all to you.

"But this - this is an old book." I glance at the paperback copy Eleanor is still clutching. "It came out five years ago."

Cassie nods, solemnly.

"We think Aloysius Hunt stole it from him, published it under his own name, and then pressured him to keep writing."

"It's true his writing changed a bit around then. Don't you remember, Merry? We talked about how his stories were all of a sudden so fresh and new - like he had a whole new lease on life."

"He was telling somebody else's stories, that's why." Eleanor's eyes flash dangerously and I again think there's a very thin line between superfan and hater, and I'm pretty sure the discovery of Aloysius Hunt's misdeeds has tipped her over the edge. "I can't believe he would do this!"

"I can." Phoebe's voice is quiet but insistent and we all turn to look at her. "He was stuck for a long time. Writer's block." She shuddered. "He became so awful to be around. Bursting into rages, then locking himself in his room for days at a time. Patrick was going mad trying to figure out how to help him." She swallows a sob. "It was my idea to show him his work. Patrick had been working on his own writing for ages and he kept putting it aside to help Mr. Hunt and I suggested one day, if his boss wasn't writing much of his own pages maybe he could help Patrick with his. Payback for all the hard work he had put in over the years." She blinks very quickly and I can tell she's determined to keep her tears at bay this time. "I'm sure once he saw how good Patrick's stories were he knew he'd found his way out. Patrick could write the stories, and Aloysius's name and fame would sell them." Her expression turns cold like steel. "And nobody would ever have to know."

"Well, they're going to know now!" Eleanor hops to her feet and is halfway out of the Jitterbug Junction before the rest of us follow her. I barely have time to close up the cafe - which is just locking the door, I don't even remember a sign this time - before we're all marching the short distance to Peter Stalker's bookstore.

There's still a queue of customers but Eleanor is a woman on a mission. She barges right to the front of the line, ignoring the protests from other shoppers, and informs Peter – telling him, not asking - that we need to speak to Aloysius Hunt right away.

"Merry?" Kate is standing just inside the door, talking to Police Chief Trainor. They both take a step towards us and I turn to explain, but before I can Aloysius Hunt spots us.

"Eleanor!" Hunt beams, pleased to see his number one fan. I glance at Cassie and we both brace for disaster once he figures out what she's really doing here.

"Mr. Hunt, I want to ask you something."

"You do?" He glances at each of us in turn, a benign smile on his face. "What's that, my dear?"

"When were you going to tell people that you haven't written a new book in years?" She holds *Death by Driving* aloft and raises her voice so that everyone in the crowded bookstore can hear her. "Every book you've published in the last five years was written by Patrick Hamilton."

"Now, hold on a minute..." Peter Stalker hurries forward, making placatory noises to encourage the rest of his customers to keep browsing. "I'm sure there's been some misunderstanding..."

"There certainly has!" Aloysius Hunt draws himself up to his full height and points a finger at Phoebe. "She is a liar! First, she sent me threatening letters and now she wants to defame my reputation! I was willing to give you a little grace, Phoebe, what with the terrible loss you've faced, but really -"

"Mr. Hunt," Kate jumps in, looking to diffuse the situation, and Chief Trainor lays a hand on her arm, wanting to diffuse *her*. None of it matters because Phoebe has summoned every ounce of courage she has. She pulls out Patrick's pages from his bag and angles them so that Aloysius Hunt - and everyone else standing near him - can see them.

"My boyfriend, Patrick Hamilton wrote this book." She points at Eleanor's copy of *Death by Driving*. "I have his proof copy right here. And on this flash drive." She pulls something else out of the bag. "I'm pretty sure we'll find drafts for every book Mr Hunt has written since then. Including his newest one."

"That's not true." Hunt's face has paled and he's shifting his weight awkwardly from side to side. "And even if it was, it would hardly be a crime. All sorts of authors use ghostwriters to help them craft a story. Even Shakespeare -"

"But Shakespeare wouldn't have killed his ghostwriter to keep him from coming clean, would he?"

• • • •

CASSIE HAS MADE THIS pronouncement - my Aunt Cassie, apparently pulling this idea out of nowhere. I turn to look at her in shock, but her idea slots neatly into the puzzle my mind has been working on all morning. *Of course. Patrick was always the target - and Aloysius Hunt was the person who stood to gain the most by his death.*

Before anyone can react, Hunt himself does. He turns suddenly, shoving people aside including Peter, who trips and falls, his head hitting the floor with a sickening thud. Hunt keeps moving, pushing people aside as he makes his way towards the door but there are too many customers and at last Chief Trainor reacts and his commanding voice is all it takes to stop Hunt in his tracks.

"Somebody call an ambulance!"

I see people standing over the prone figure of Peter Stalker and feel my stomach lurch.

"He's ok." Another person has dropped to their knees next to him and is taking his pulse. "He's just unconscious."

Kate appears beside us, a glance at her boss confirming he has Aloysius Hunt secured. Over the hustle and bustle of bystanders, I hear her voice, calm and confident.

"Can you three come with us to the police station? I think we need to get a few things straightened out."

And that's how I end up in an interrogation room with Phoebe, who is white-faced and silent, and my Aunt Cassie, who has more than enough to say for all three of us.

"It's ingenious if you think about it, which of course I have been doing, non-stop. I just couldn't understand why anyone would want poor Patrick out of the way." She glances at me. "I'm sorry to say my suspicions landed on Phoebe here for a little while."

"What?"

Phoebe turns wide-eyed to look at Cassie, but I'm more vocal in my shock.

"You thought Phoebe might have had something to do with it all?"

"Well, she did, didn't she? The letters."

"But I didn't -" Phoebe stammers. "I never would have -"

"Oh, I know that now, dear." Cassie leans across me and pats Phoebe warmly on the arm. "But at the time I couldn't be sure. So I decided it was best to keep you close enough for observation, and where better than under my own roof?"

"My roof, actually," I put in, wondering if Cassie has any understanding of just how much danger we could have been in if she'd been right. "I can't believe you thought Phoebe was a murderer."

"Potential murderer," Cassie corrects me. "And I never said I thought that. Only that she might have been involved. It seemed a bit strange to me how everyone leaped to the conclusion that Aloysius Hunt was the intended victim all along, you see. Why couldn't poor Patrick have been the one in danger? Maybe he had enemies of his own." She sighs. "I just couldn't figure out who, or why they would want to go to the trouble of killing him in such a cruel way."

"It was supposed to look like an accident," Kate says.

"Oh, but it wasn't." Cassie shook her head. "Don't you see? That's the whole point. It was an idea ripped straight from the pages of a book. At first, that seemed to fit the idea of Aloysius Hunt having a stalker who was tormenting him with unkind letters." Again she leans across me and pats Phoebe's arm. "And mimicking the disasters he himself wrote about, well." She sucks in a breath. "But when it turned out that Hunt never even wrote that - that Patrick did?" She shrugs her shoulders. "It's quite clear that Hunt was behind it all. I expect Patrick was getting tired of being his ghostwriter and wanted to publish his own books under his own name. Maybe even come clean about who had really been writing Aloysius Hunt's latest bestsellers. Hunt couldn't have that."

Kate is furiously jotting down notes as Cassie talks and eventually she looks up, her lips quirking as she fights a smile.

"Well, Cassie. You seem to have done my job for me and solved the crime quite easily. Any chance I can persuade you to stick around in Silver Brook and solve a few more?"

Cassie looks at me, her eyes bright with mischief.

"I'm sure I don't need to. Not when you have my niece here. I only wanted to try my hand at it." She shivered. "No, I'll be quite happy to go back home again and leave all this murder business confined to the pages of a book.

A day or two later - it could been weeks for all the change that's happened - I'm at work in the Jitterbug Junction and I finally have some help.

"Like this?"

Phoebe tilts the milk jug one way then another, arranging the foam on the top of her first latte in an array of patterned swirls that I try not to envy. Her skill at calligraphy has easily transferred into making latte art and her first attempt is better than my fiftieth.

"Beautiful!" I say and mean it. She beams at me, then hands the drink to Jeremy, who takes it with a smile before crossing the cafe and joining Kate and Cassie at one of a few empty tables. Business is humming along but it's not so busy I can't take a break to join my friends. I leave Phoebe in charge, grateful to have some support at last, and totter after Jeremy, arriving just in time to catch the end of Kate's comments.

"We were worried about getting him to talk in the first place but now it's going to be a challenge just to get him to shut up." She rolls her eyes. "He's already talking about writing his memoir."

"That is one book I certainly don't intend to read." Cassie purses her lips in distaste. "I knew I didn't like that man the very first time I saw him." She glances up at me. "Oh, Merry, dear, come sit with us."

"Your new helper seems to be settling in well!" Jeremy tilts his latte, admiring the pattern in the foam. "Is she going to stick around?"

"I hope so."

Phoebe isn't staying at my house anymore, but she certainly can't live long-term at the Harmony Inn. I'm going to check out a few rentals with her at the weekend in hopes we can find her the perfect place.

"This is going to be just the fresh start she needs," Cassie remarks, looking rather satisfied with the way things have all turned out. "You get a new assistant she gets a new job. Perfect."

"Apart from Patrick not being here to share it all with her." Kate's comment brings everybody down and there's a long silence before Jeremy clears his throat and breaks it.

"So how's Jim handling things?" *Jim* is Police Chief Trainor. I glance at Kate and watch her roll her eyes.

"He's acting like he knew Aloysius Hunt was responsible all along." Her features pinch and she lowers the pitch of her voice, mimicking Trainor's. "That's why I was determined to stay so close, Kelly. I was just waiting for him to make a wrong move. And it all worked out, didn't it? I was right there, on the scene."

"So were you!" I protest but Kate shakes her head. She's been battling the Trainor-shaped obstacle to career advancement in the Silver Brook police force for several years now and I guess she knows how to handle him.

"I'm just glad he's the one who had to take Hunt's statements. Once we got him to admit to the crime he can't stop talking about it. I think he's eager for everyone to know just how smart he was to set everything up the way he did."

"Not smart enough to get away with it though," Cassie sniffs.

"He just didn't reckon on you being in town at the same time he was," I say, sliding my arm around her and hugging her. "I'm glad you were."

"So am I!" Cassie's stern frown slips into her more familiar smile and her eyes sparkle as she looks at me. "Although I certainly won't regret going home again. Silver Brook is a charming little town but I'm beginning to think you have a few too many murders for one to ever feel truly comfortable here. Not like Patterson, where the worst crime is not putting enough chairs out at the local town meeting."

· · · ·

LIFE IS A LOT QUIETER after Cassie goes home, although she makes me promise to go and visit her in Patterson before too long.

"And bring that handsome young man of yours too! I still can't believe he wasn't around for me to meet him yet!"

Rob is disappointed too, and he laughs as Phoebe and I tell him everything Cassie said in her parting speech.

"Well, I'm glad you're still here, Phoebe," he says, admiring the elegant coffee she pours into a takeaway cup as he comes to pick me up for an afternoon off. It's the first proper break from work I've had since taking on the Jitterbug Junction, and I can't help but feel grateful for my new co-worker, even if I regret the death that brought her here.

"Me too!" she says, with a smile. "I love it here. Everyone is so friendly!"

"See if you still think that way once you mess up someone's very detailed and very specific order." I wince. "For the third time."

We all laugh, and with one last glance around the cafe to check I'm not leaving Phoebe with too many customers to take care of, Rob and I step out into the afternoon sun. He's been telling me all about his exotic animals conference and then demands to hear, again, the story of Aloysius Hunt and his deadly Silver Brook book launch.

"I know at least a few people who are excited to revisit it," I say, recalling a visit I had the previous day from Jessica and her true-crime podcast pals. "So you'll be able to listen to every excruciating detail on Sleuthing Silver Brook."

"True!" He slips an arm around my shoulder as we continue our progress down the high street towards Peter Stalker's bookstore. Business is thriving and Rob and I spot the crowds even before we venture inside.

"Merry!" Peter rushes over to greet us, looking more cheerful than I've ever seen him. I can still see the faint outline of a bruise and wonder if the blow to his head contributed to his change in temperament, or if that's solely a result of his business improving.

"You've made a few changes around here," I say, pointing to a couple of new bookshelves displaying a choice of books that gets swiftly picked over by customers. "I'm glad business is doing well."

"Better than well! Ever since - well, you know." He chuckles. "And I do take great delight in telling everyone that the actual body in the bookstore was me! Although, ho ho, I was only just knocked unconscious." He taps his head knowingly. "Right over there!" He points to the spot where he fell and I see the shape of a sprawling body outlined in white tape, just like at a crime scene.

Rob grins at me.

"I'm pleased to see you're capitalizing on the incident, Mr. Stalker."

"Peter!" Peter barks. "Call me Peter. But you're quite right. My footfall is up across the board. Lots more customers, lots more sales." His gaze travels to me and he grins. "I'm even starting a new crime-solving book club - the Tuesday Night "Whodunnits". You'll join, won't you, Merry? We could do with adding someone with your expertise to our ranks."

"I'll think about it," I promise, exchanging a glance with Rob. "Although I think I've had enough of murder for a little while."

· · · ·

The End

About the Author

When Rachel Beattie isn't writing stories, she's usually reading them - especially of the cozy mystery variety. A lifelong devotee of Agatha Christie, she loves putting ze little grey cells to work and is especially fond of anything that can make her laugh while she's collecting a clue or two.

• • • •

Join her mailing list[1] for more information, new release news, exclusives and bonus content.

---

1. https://mailchi.mp/003ddbbcc668/newsletter-subscribers

Also by Rachel Beattie

A Serenity Suites Cozy Mystery
Cassie Clinton and the First Fatality
Double Trouble for Cassie Clinton
Cassie Clinton and the Triple Threat

A Slice of Life Cozy Mystery
Love, Lies and Pumpkin Spice
Wed, Dead and Gingerbread
Crime Scenes and Blackcurrant Cream
Spirits, Spells and Caramel
Broken Hearts and Strawberry Tarts
Black Tie and Vanilla Pie
A Slice of Life Cozy Mystery Books 1-3

A Very Merry Murder Mystery
The Santa Slaughter
The First Date Disaster
The Body in the Bookstore

The Harmony Inn Homicide
The Scandal at the Spa
The Babysitter Bungle
The Campground Killer
The Deadly Dinner Party
The Flower Shop Felony
A Very Merry Murder Mystery Books 1-3

www.ingramcontent.com/pod-product-compliance
Lightning Source LLC
Chambersburg PA
CBHW031456130726
47989CB00003B/1418